The Well of Pen-Morfa

Elizabeth Gaskell

CHAPTER I

Of a hundred travellers who spend a night at Tre-Madoc, in North Wales, there is not one, perhaps, who goes to the neighbouring village of Pen-Morfa. The new town, built by Mr Maddocks, Shelley's friend, has taken away all the importance of the ancient village—formerly, as its name imports, 'the head of the marsh;' that marsh which Mr Maddocks drained and dyked, and reclaimed from the Traeth Mawr, till Pen-Morfa, against the walls of whose cottages the winter tides lashed in former days, has come to stand, high and dry, three miles from the sea, on a disused road to Caernarvon. I do not think there has been a new cottage built in Pen-Morfa this hundred years, and many an old one has dates in some obscure corner which tell of the fifteenth century. The joists of timber, where they meet overhead, are blackened with the smoke of centuries. There is one large room, round which the beds are built like cupboards, with wooden doors to open and shut, somewhat in the old Scotch fashion, I imagine; and below the bed (at least in one instance I can testify that this was the case, and I was told it was not uncommon) is a great wide wooden drawer, which contained the oat-cake, baked for some months' consumption by the family. They call the promontory of Llyn (the point at the end of Caernarvonshire), *Welsh Wales*. I think they might call Pen-Morfa a Welsh Welsh village; it is so national in its ways, and buildings, and inhabitants, and so different from the towns and hamlets into which the English throng in summer. How these said inhabitants of Pen-Morfa ever are distinguished by their names, I, uninitiated, cannot tell. I only know for a fact, that in a family there with which I am acquainted, the eldest son's name is John Jones, because his father's was John Thomas; that the second son is called David Williams, because his grandfather was William Wynn; and that the girls are called indiscriminately by the names of Thomas and Jones. I have heard some of the Welsh chuckle over the way in which they have baffled the barristers at Caernarvon assizes, denying the name under which they had been subpoenaed to give evidence, if they were unwilling witnesses. I could tell you of a great deal which is peculiar and wild in these true Welsh people, who are what I suppose we English were a century ago; but I must hasten on to my tale.

I have received great, true, beautiful kindness from one of the members of the family of whom I just now spoke as living at Pen-Morfa; and when I found that they wished me to drink tea with them, I gladly did so, though my friend was the only one in the house who could speak English at all fluently. After tea, I went with them to see some of their friends; and it was then I saw the interiors of the houses of which I have spoken. It was an autumn evening: we left mellow sunset-light in the open air when we entered the houses, in which all seemed dark, save in the ruddy sphere of the firelight, for the windows were very' small, and deep-set in the thick walls. Here were an old couple, who welcomed me in Welsh; and brought forth milk and oat-cake with patriarchal hospitality. Sons and daughters had married away from them; they lived alone; he was blind, or nearly so; and they sat one on each side of the fire, so old and so still (till we went in and broke the silence) that they seemed to be listening for death. At another house lived a woman stern and severe-looking. She was busy hiving a swarm of bees, alone and unassisted. I do not think my companion would have chosen to speak to her; but seeing her out in her hill-side garden, she made some inquiry in Welsh, which was answered in the most mournful tone I ever heard in my life; a voice of which the freshness and 'timbre' had been choked up by tears long years ago. I asked who she was. I dare say the story is common enough; but the sight of the woman and her few words had impressed me. She had been the beauty of Pen-Morfa; had been in service; had been taken to London by the family whom she served; had come down, in a year or so, back to Pen-Morfa, her beauty gone into that sad, wild, despairing look which I saw; and she about to become a mother. Her father had died during her absence, and left her a very little money; and after her child was born, she took the little cottages where I saw her, and made a scanty living by the produce of her bees. She associated with no one. One event had made her savage and distrustful to her kind. She kept so much aloof that it was some time before it became known that her child was deformed, and had lost the use of its lower limbs. Poor thing! When I saw the mother, it had been for fifteen years bedridden. But go past when you would, in the night, you saw a light burning; it was often that of the watching mother, solitary and friendless, soothing the moaning child; or you might hear her crooning some old Welsh air, in hopes to still the pain with the loud monotonous music. Her sorrow was so dignified, and her mute endurance and her patient love won her such

3

respect, that the neighbours would fain have been friends; but she kept alone and solitary. This a most true story. I hope that woman and her child are dead now, and their souls above.

Another story which I heard of these old primitive dwellings I mean to tell at somewhat greater length:—

There are rocks high above Pen-Morfa; they are the same that hang over Tre-Madoc, but near Pen-Morfa they sweep away, and are lost in the plain. Everywhere they are beautiful. The great, sharp ledges, which would otherwise look hard and cold, are adorned with the brightest-coloured moss, and the golden lichen. Close to, you see the scarlet leaves of the crane's-bill, and the tufts of purple heather, which fill up every cleft and cranny; but, in the distance, you see only the general effect of infinite richness of colour, broken, here and there, by great masses of ivy. At the foot of these rocks come a rich, verdant meadow or two; and then you are at Pen-Morfa. The village well is sharp down under the rocks. There are one or two large sloping pieces of stone in that last field, on the road leading to the well, which are always slippery; slippery in the summer's heat, almost as much as in the frost of winter, when some little glassy stream that runs over them is turned into a thin sheet of ice. Many, many years back—a lifetime ago—there lived in Pen-Morfa a widow and her daughter. Very little is required in those out-of-the-way Welsh villages. The wants of the people are very simple. Shelter, fire, a little oat-cake and buttermilk, and garden produce; perhaps some pork and bacon from the pig in winter; clothing,

4

which is principally of home manufacture, and of the most enduring kind: these take very little money to purchase, especially in a district into which the large capitalists have not yet come, to buy up two or three acres of the peasants; and nearly every man about Pen-Morfa owned, at the time of which I speak, his dwelling and some land beside.

Eleanor Gwynn inherited the cottage (by the roadside, on the left hand as you go from Tre-Madoc to Pen-Morfa) in which she and her husband had lived all their married life, and a small garden sloping southwards, in which her bees lingered before winging their way to the more distant heather. She took rank among her neighbours as the possessor of a moderate independence—not rich, and not poor. But the young men of Pen-Morfa thought her very rich in the possession of a most lovely daughter. Most of us know how very pretty Welsh women are; but, from all accounts Nest Gwynn (Nest, or Nesta, is the Welsh for Agnes) was more regularly beautiful than any one for miles round. The Welsh are still fond of triads, and 'as beautiful as a summer's morning at sunrise, as a white seagull on the green sea wave, and as Nest Gwynn,' is yet a saying in that district. Nest knew she was beautiful, and delighted in it. Her mother sometimes checked her in her happy pride, and sometimes reminded her that beauty was a great gift of God (for the Welsh are a very pious people); but when she began her little homily, Nest came dancing to her, and knelt down before her, and put her face up to be kissed, and so, with a sweet interruption, she stopped her mother's lips. Her high spirits made some few shake their heads, and some called her a flirt and a coquette; for she could not help trying to please all, both old and young, both men and women. A very little from Nest sufficed for this; a sweet, glittering smile, a word of kindness, a merry glance, or a little sympathy; all these pleased and attracted: she was like the fairy-gifted child, and dropped inestimable gifts. But some, who had interpreted her smiles and kind words rather as their wishes led them, than as they were really warranted, found that the beautiful, beaming Nest could be decided and saucy enough; and so they revenged themselves by calling her a flirt. Her mother heard it, and sighed; but Nest only laughed.

It was her work to fetch water for the day's use from the well I told you about. Old people say it was the prettiest sight in the world to see her come stepping lightly and gingerly over the stones with the pail of water balanced on her head; she was too adroit to need to steady it with her hand. They say, now that they can afford to be charitable and speak the truth, that in all her changes to other people, there never was a better daughter to a widowed mother than Nest. There is a picturesque old farmhouse under Moel Gwynn, on the road from Tre-Madoc to Criccaeth, called by some Welsh name which I now forget; but its meaning in English is 'The End of Time;' a strange, boding, ominous name. Perhaps, the builder meant his work to endure till the end of time. I do not know; but there the old house stands, and will stand for many a year. When Nest was young, it belonged to one Edward Williams; his mother was dead, and people said he was on the look-out for a wife. They told Nest so, but she tossed her head and reddened, and said she thought he might look long before he got one; so it was not strange that one morning when she went to the well, one autumn morning when the dew lay heavy on the grass, and the thrushes were busy among the mountain-ash berries, Edward Williams happened to be there, on his way to the coursing match near, and somehow his greyhounds threw her pail of water over in their romping play, and she was very long in filling it again; and when she came home she threw her arms round her mother's neck, and, in a passion of joyous tears, told her that Edward Williams, of 'The End of Time,' had asked her to marry him, and that she had said 'Yes.'

Eleanor Gwynn shed her tears too; but they fell quietly when she was alone. She was thankful Nest had found a protector—one suitable in age and apparent character, and above her in fortune; but she knew she should miss her sweet daughter in a thousand household ways; miss her in the evenings by the fireside; miss her when at night she wakened up with a start from a dream of her youth, and saw her fair face lying calm in the moonlight, pillowed by her side. Then she forgot her dream, and blessed her child, and slept again. But who could be so selfish as to be sad when Nest was so supremely happy; she danced and sang more than ever; and then sat silent, and smiled to herself: if spoken to, she started and came back to the present with a scarlet blush, which told what she had been thinking of.

That was a sunny, happy, enchanted autumn. But the winter was nigh at hand; and with it came sorrow. One fine frosty morning, Nest went out with her lover—she to the well, he to some farming business, which was to be transacted at the little inn of Pen-Morfa. He was late for his appointment; so he left her at the entrance of the village, and hastened to the inn; and she, in her best cloak and new hat (put on against her mother's advice; but they were a recent purchase, and very becoming), went through the Dol Mawr, radiant with love and happiness. One who lived until lately, met her going down towards the well that morning, and said 'he turned round to look' after her—she seemed unusually lovely. He wondered at the time at her wearing her Sunday clothes; for the pretty, hooded blue-cloth cloak is kept among the Welsh women as a church and market garment, and not commonly used, even on the coldest days of winter, for such household errands as fetching water from the well. However, as he said, 'It was not possible to look in her face, and "fault" anything she wore.' Down the sloping stones the girl went blithely with her pail. She filled it at the well; and then she took off her hat, tied the strings together, and slung it over her arm. She lifted the heavy pail and balanced it on her head. But, alas! in going up the smooth, slippery, treacherous rock, the encumbrance of her cloak—it might be such a trifle as her slung hat—something, at any rate, took away her evenness of poise; the freshet had frozen on the slanting stone, and was one coat of ice; poor Nest fell, and put out her hip. No more flushing rosy colour on that sweet face; no more look of beaming innocent happiness; instead, there was deadly pallor, and filmy eyes, over which dark shades seemed to chase each other as the shoots of agony grew more and more intense. She screamed once or twice; but the exertion (involuntary, and forced out of her by excessive pain) overcame her, and she fainted. A child, coming an hour or two afterwards, on the same errand, saw her lying there, ice-glued to the stone, and thought she was dead. It flew crying back.

'Nest Gwynn is dead! Nest Gwynn is dead!' and, crazy with fear, it did not stop until it had hid its head in its mother's lap. The village was alarmed, and all who were able went in haste towards the well. Poor Nest had often thought she was dying in that dreary hour; had taken fainting for death, and struggled against it; and prayed that God would keep her alive till she could see her lover's face once more; and when she did see it, white with terror, bending over her, she gave a feeble smile, and let herself faint away into unconsciousness.

Many a month she lay on her bed unable to move. Sometimes she was delirious, sometimes worn-out into the deepest depression. Through all, her mother watched her with tenderest care. The neighbours would come and offer help. They would bring presents of country dainties; and I do not suppose that there was a better dinner than ordinary cooked in any household in Pen-Morfa parish, but a portion of it was sent to Eleanor Gwynn, if not for her sick daughter, to try and tempt her herself to eat and' be strengthened; for to no one would she delegate the duty of watching over her child. Edward Williams was for a long time most assiduous in his inquiries and attentions; but by-and-by (ah! you see the dark fate of poor Nest now), he slackened, so little at first that Eleanor blamed herself for her jealousy on her daughter's behalf, and chid her suspicious heart. But as spring ripened into summer, and Nest was still bedridden, Edward's coolness was visible to more than the poor mother. The neighbours would have spoken to her about it, but she shrunk from the subject as if they were probing a wound. 'At any rate,' thought she, 'Nest shall be strong before she is told about it. I will tell lies—I shall be forgiven—but I must save my child; and when she is stronger, perhaps I may be able to comfort her. Oh! I wish she would not speak to him so tenderly and trustfully, when she is delirious. I could curse him when she does.' And then Nest would call for her mother, and Eleanor would go and invent some strange story about the summonses Edward had had to Caernarvon assizes, or to Harlech cattle market. But at last she was driven to her wits' end; it was three weeks since he had even stopped at the door to inquire, and Eleanor, mad with anxiety about her child, who was silently pining off to death for want of tidings of her lover, put on her cloak, when she had lulled her daughter to sleep one fine June evening, and set off to 'The End of Time.' The great plain which stretches out like an amphitheatre, in the half-circle of hills formed by the ranges of Moel Gwynn and the Tre-Madoc Rocks, was all golden-green in the mellow light of sunset. To Eleanor it might have been black with winter frost—she never noticed outward things till she reached 'The End of Time;' and there, in the little farm-yard, she was brought to a sense of her present hour and errand by seeing Edward. He was examining some hay, newly stacked; the air was scented by its fragrance, and by the lingering sweetness of the breath of the cows. When Edward turned round at the footstep and saw

Eleanor, he coloured and looked confused; however, he came forward to meet her in a cordial manner enough.

'It's a fine evening,' said he. 'How is Nest? But, indeed, your being here is a sign she is better. Won't you come in and sit down?' He spoke hurriedly, as if affecting a welcome which he did not feel.

'Thank you. I'll just take this milking-stool and sit down here. The open air is like balm, after being shut up so long.'

'It is a long time,' he replied, 'more than five months.'

Mrs Gwynn was trembling at heart. She felt an anger which she did not wish to show; for, if by any manifestations of temper or resentment she lessened or broke the waning thread of attachment which bound him to her daughter, she felt she should never forgive herself. She kept inwardly saying, 'Patience, patience! he may be true, and love her yet;' but her indignant convictions gave her words the lie.

'It's a long time, Edward Williams, since you've been near us to ask after Nest,' said she. 'She may be better, or she may be worse, for aught you know.' She looked up at him reproachfully, but spoke in a gentle, quiet tone.

'I—you see the hay has been a long piece of work. The weather has been fractious—and a master's eye is needed. Besides,' said he, as if he had found the reason for which he sought to account for his absence, 'I have heard of her from Rowland Jones. I was at the surgery for

11

some horse-medicine—he told me about her:' and a shade came over his face, as he remembered what the doctor had said. Did he think that shade would escape the mother's eye?

'You saw Rowland Jones! Oh, man-alive, tell me what he said of my girl! He'll say nothing to me, but just hems and haws the more I pray him. But you will tell me. You *must* tell me.' She stood up and spoke in a tone of command, which his feeling of independence, weakened just then by an accusing conscience, did not enable him to resist. He strove to evade the question, however.

'It was an unlucky day that ever she went to the well!'

'Tell me what the doctor said of my child,' repeated Mrs Gwynn. 'Will she live, or will she die?' He did not dare to disobey the imperious tone in which this question was put.

'Oh, she will live, don't be afraid. The doctor said she would live.' He did not mean to lay any peculiar emphasis on the word 'live,' but somehow he did, and she, whose every nerve vibrated with anxiety, caught the word.

'She will live!' repeated she. 'But there is something behind. Tell me, for I will know. If you won't say, I'll go to Rowland Jones to-night, and make him tell me what he has said to you.'

There had passed something in this conversation between himself and the doctor, which Edward did not wish to have known; and Mrs Gwynn's threat had the desired effect. But he looked vexed and irritated.

'You have such impatient ways with you, Mrs Gwynn,' he remonstrated.

'I am a mother asking news of my sick child,' said she. 'Go on. What did he say? She'll live—' as if giving the clue.

'She'll live, he has no doubt of that. But he thinks—now don't clench your hands so—I can't tell you if you look in that way; you are enough to frighten a man.'

'I'm not speaking,' said she, in a low, husky tone. 'Never mind my looks: she'll live——'

'But she'll be a cripple for life. There! you would have it out,' said he, sulkily.

'A cripple for life,' repeated she, slowly. 'And I'm one-and-twenty years older than she is!' She sighed heavily.

'And, as we're about it, I'll just tell you what is in my mind,' said he, hurried and confused. 'I've a deal of cattle; and the farm makes heavy work, as much as an able healthy woman can do. So you see——' He stopped, wishing her to understand his meaning without words. But she would not. She fixed her dark eyes on him, as if reading his soul, till he flinched under her gaze.

'Well,' said she, at length, 'say on. Remember, I've a deal of work in me yet, and what strength is mine is my daughter's.'

'You're very good. But, altogether, you must be aware, Nest will never be the same as she was.'

'And you've not yet sworn in the face of God to take, her for better, for worse; and, as she is worse'—she looked in his face, caught her breath, and went on—'as she is worse, why, you cast her off, not being church-tied to her. Though her body may be crippled, her poor heart is the same—alas!—and full of love for you. Edward, you don't mean to break it off because of our sorrows. You're only trying me, I know,' said she, as if begging him to assure her that her fears were false. 'But, you see, I'm a foolish woman—a poor, foolish woman—and ready to take fright at a few words.' She smiled up in his face; but it was a forced, doubting smile, and his face still retained its sullen, dogged aspect.

'Nay, Mrs Gwynn,' said he, 'you spoke truth at first. Your own good sense told you Nest would never be fit to be any man's wife—unless, indeed, she could catch Mr Griffiths of Tynwntyrybwlch; he might keep her a carriage, maybe.' Edward really did not mean to be unfeeling; but he was obtuse, and wished to carry off his 'embarrassment by a kind of friendly joke, which he had no idea would sting the poor mother as it did. He was startled at her manner.

'Put it in words like a man. Whatever you mean by my child, say it for yourself, and don't speak as if my good sense had told me anything. I stand here, doubting my own thoughts, cursing my own fears. Don't be a coward. I ask you whether you and Nest are troth-plight?'

'I am not a coward. Since you ask me, I answer, Nest and I *were* troth-plight; but we *are* not. I cannot—no one would expect me to wed a cripple. It's your own doing I've told you now; I had made up my mind, but I should have waited a bit before telling you.'

'Very well,' said she, and she turned to go away; but her wrath burst the flood-gates, and swept away discretion and forethought. She moved, and stood in the gateway. Her lips parted, but no sound came; with an hysterical motion, she threw her arms suddenly up to heaven, as if bringing down lightning towards the grey old house to which she pointed as they fell, and then she spoke—

'The widow's child is unfriended. As surely as the Saviour brought the son of a widow from death to life, for her tears and cries, so surely will God and His angels watch over my Nest, and avenge her cruel wrongs.' She turned away weeping, and wringing her hands.

Edward went in-doors; he had no more desire to reckon his stores; he sat by the fire, looking gloomily at the red ashes. He might have been there half an hour or more, when some one knocked at the door. He would not speak. He wanted no one's company. Another knock, sharp and loud. He did not speak. Then the visitor opened the door, and, to his surprise—almost to his affright—Eleanor Gwynn came in.

'I knew you were here. I knew you could not go out into the clear, holy night as if nothing had happened. Oh! did I curse you? If I did, I beg you to forgive me; and I will try and ask the Almighty to bless you, if you will but have a little mercy—a very little. It will kill my Nest if she knows the truth now—she is so very weak. Why, she cannot feed herself, she is so low and feeble. You would not wish to kill her, I think, Edward!' She looked at him, as if expecting an answer; but he did not speak. She went down on her knees on the flags by him.

'You will give me a little time, Edward, to get her strong, won't you, now? I ask it on my bended knees! Perhaps, if I promise never to curse you again, you will come sometimes to see her, till she is well enough to know how all is over, and her heart's hopes crushed. Only say you'll come for a month or so, as if you still loved her—the poor cripple, forlorn of the world. I'll get her strong, and not tax you long.' Her tears fell too fast for her to go on.

'Get up, Mrs Gwynn,' Edward said. 'Don't kneel to me. I have no objection to come and see Nest, now and then, so that all is clear between you and me. Poor thing! I'm sorry, as it happens, she's so taken up with the thought of me.'

'It was likely, was not it? and you to have been her husband before this time, if—oh, miserable me! to let my child go and dim her bright life! But you'll forgive me, and come sometimes, just for a little quarter of an hour, once or twice a week. Perhaps she'll be asleep sometimes when you call, and then, you know, you need not come in. If she were not so ill, I'd never ask you.'

So low and humble was the poor widow brought, through her exceeding love for her daughter.

CHAPTER II

Nest revived during the warm summer weather. Edward came to see her, and stayed the allotted quarter of an hour; but he dared not look her in the face. She was, indeed, a cripple: one leg was much shorter than the other, and she halted on a crutch. Her face, formerly so brilliant in colour, was wan and pale with suffering; the bright roses were gone, never to return. Her large eyes were sunk deep down in their hollow, cavernous sockets; but the light was in them still, when Edward came. Her mother dreaded her returning strength—dreaded, yet desired it; for the heavy burden of her secret was most oppressive at times, and she thought Edward was beginning to weary of his enforced attentions. One October evening she told her the truth. She even compelled her rebellious heart to take the cold, reasoning side of the question; and she told her child that her disabled frame was a disqualification for ever becoming a farmer's wife. She spoke hardly, because her inner agony and sympathy was such, she dared not trust herself to express the feelings that were rending her. But Nest turned away from cold reason; she revolted from her mother; she revolted from the world. She bound her sorrow tight up in her breast, to corrode and fester there.

Night after night, her mother heard her cries and moans—more pitiful, by far, than those wrung from her by bodily pain a year before; and night after night, if her mother spoke to soothe, she proudly denied the existence of any pain but what was physical, and consequent upon her accident.

'If she would but open her sore heart to me—to me, her mother,' Eleanor wailed forth in prayer to God, 'I would be content. Once it was enough to have my Nest all my own. Then came love, and I knew it would never be as before; and then I thought the grief I felt, when Edward spoke to me, was as sharp a sorrow as could be; but this present grief, 0 Lord, my God, is worst of all; and Thou only, Thou, canst help!'

When Nest grew as strong as she was ever likely to be on earth, she was anxious to have as much labour as she could bear. She would not allow her mother to spare her anything. Hard work—bodily fatigue—she seemed to crave. She was glad when she was stunned by exhaustion into a dull insensibility of feeling. She was almost fierce when her mother, in those first months of convalescence, performed the household tasks which had formerly been hers; but she shrank from going out of doors. Her mother thought that she was unwilling to expose her changed appearance to the neighbours' remarks, but Nest was not afraid of that; she was afraid of their pity, as being one deserted and cast off. If Eleanor gave way before her daughter's imperiousness, and sat by while Nest 'tore' about her work with the vehemence of a bitter heart, Eleanor could have cried, but she durst not; tears, or any mark of commiseration, irritated the crippled girl so much, she even drew away from caresses. Everything was to go on as it had been before she had known Edward; and so it did, outwardly; but they trod carefully, as if the ground on which they moved was hollow—deceptive. There was no more careless ease, every word was guarded, and every action planned. It was a dreary life to both. Once, Eleanor brought in a little baby, a neighbour's child, to try and tempt Nest out of herself, by her old love of children. Nest's pale face flushed as she saw the innocent child in her mother's arms; and, for a moment, she made as if she would have taken it; but then she turned away, and hid her face behind her apron, and murmured, 'I shall never have a child to lie in my breast, and call me mother!' In a minute she arose, with compressed and tightened lips, and went about her household work, without her noticing the cooing baby again, till Mrs Gwynn, heart-sick at the failure of her little plan, took it back to its parents.

One day the news ran through Pen-Morfa that Edward Williams was about to be married. Eleanor had long expected this intelligence. It came upon her like no new thing, but it was the filling-up of her cup of woe. She could not tell Nest. She sat listlessly in the house, and dreaded that each neighbour who came in would speak about the village news. At last some one did. Nest looked round from her employment, and talked of the event with a kind of cheerful curiosity as to the particulars, which made her informant go away, and tell others that Nest had quite left off caring for Edward Williams. But when the door was shut, and Eleanor and she were left alone, Nest came and stood before her weeping mother like a stern accuser.

'Mother, why did not you let me die? Why did you keep me alive for this?' Eleanor could not speak, but she put her arms out towards her girl. Nest turned away, and Eleanor cried aloud in her soreness of spirit. Nest came again.

'Mother, I was wrong. You did your best. I don't know how it is I am so hard and cold. I wish I had died when I was a girl, and had a feeling heart.'

'Don't speak so, my child. God has afflicted you sore, and your hardness of heart is but for a time. Wait a little. Don't reproach yourself, my poor Nest. I understand your ways. I don't mind them, love. The feeling heart will come back to you in time. Anyways, don't think you're grieving me; because, love, that may sting you when I'm gone; and I'm not grieved, my darling. Most times, we're very cheerful, I think.'

After this, mother and child were drawn more together. But Eleanor had received her death from, these sorrowful, hurrying events. She did not conceal the truth from herself, nor did she pray to live, as some months ago she had done, for her child's sake; she had found out that she had no power to console the poor wounded heart. It seemed to her as if her prayers had been of no avail; and then she blamed herself for this thought.

There are many Methodist preachers in this part of Wales. There was a certain old man, named David Hughes, who was held in peculiar reverence because he had known the great John Wesley. He had been captain of a Caernarvon slate-vessel; he had traded in the Mediterranean, and had seen strange sights. In those early days (to use his own expression) he had lived without God in the world; but he went to mock John Wesley, and was converted by the white-haired patriarch, and remained to pray. Afterwards he became one of the earnest, self-denying, much-abused band of itinerant preachers who went forth under Wesley's direction, to spread abroad a more earnest and practical spirit of religion. His rambles and travels were of use to him. They extended his knowledge of the circumstances in which men are sometimes placed, and enlarged his sympathy with the tried and tempted. His sympathy, combined with the thoughtful experience of fourscore years, made him cognizant of many of the strange secrets of humanity; and when younger preachers upbraided the hard hearts they met with, and despaired of the sinners, he 'suffered long, and was kind.'

When Eleanor Gwynn lay low on her death-bed, David Hughes came to Pen-Morfa. He knew her history, and sought her out. To him she imparted the feelings I have described.

'I have lost my faith, David. The tempter has come, and I have yielded. I doubt if my prayers have been heard. Day and night have I prayed that I might comfort my child in her great sorrow; but God has not heard me. She has turned away from me, and refused my poor love. I wish to die now; but I have lost my faith, and have no more pleasure in the thought of going to God. What must I do, David?'

She hung upon his answer; and it was long in coming.

'I am weary of earth,' said she, mournfully, 'and can I find rest in death even, leaving my child desolate and broken-hearted?'

'Eleanor,' said David, 'where you go, all things will be made clear; and you will learn to thank God for the end of what now seems grievous and heavy to be borne. Do you think your agony has been greater than the awful agony in the Garden—or your prayers more earnest than that which He prayed in that hour when the great drops of blood ran down his face like sweat? We know that God heard Him, although no answer came to Him through the dread silence of that night. God's times are not our times. I have lived eighty and one years, and never yet have I known an earnest prayer fall to the ground unheeded. In an unknown way, and when no one looked for it, maybe, the answer came; a fuller, more satisfying answer than heart could conceive of, although it might be different to what was expected. Sister, you are going where in His light you will see light; you will learn there that in very faithfulness he has afflicted you!'

'Go on—you strengthen me,' said she.

After David Hughes left that day, Eleanor was calm as one already dead, and past mortal strife. Nest was awed by the change. No more passionate weeping—no more sorrow in the voice; though it was low and weak, it sounded with a sweet composure. Her last look was a smile; her last word a blessing.

Nest, tearless, streaked the poor worn body. She laid a plate with salt upon it on the breast, and lighted candles for the head and feet. It was an old Welsh custom; but when David Hughes came in, the sight carried him back to the time when he had seen the chapels in some old Catholic cathedral. Nest sat gazing on the dead with dry, hot eyes.

'She is dead,' said David, solemnly; 'she died in Christ. Let us bless God, my child. He giveth and He taketh away.'

'She is dead,' said Nest, 'my mother is dead. No one loves me now.

She spoke as if she were thinking aloud, for she did not look at David, or ask him to be seated.

'No one loves you now? No human creature, you mean. You are not yet fit to be spoken to concerning God's infinite love. I, like you, will speak of love for human creatures. I tell you if no one loves you, it is time for you to begin to love.' He spoke almost severely (if David Hughes ever did); for, to tell the truth, he was repelled by her hard rejection of her mother's tenderness, about which the neighbours had told him.

'Begin to love!' said she, her eyes flashing. 'Have I not loved? Old man, you are dim, and worn-out. You do not remember what love is.' She spoke with a scornful kind of pitying endurance. 'I will tell you how I have loved by telling you the change it has wrought in me. I was once the beautiful Nest Gwynn; I am now a cripple, a poor, wan-faced cripple, old before my time. That is a change, at least people think so.' She paused and then spoke lower. 'I tell you, David Hughes, that outward change is as nothing compared to the change in my nature caused by the love I have felt—and have had rejected. I was gentle once, and if you spoke a tender word, my heart came towards you as natural as a little child goes to its mammy. I never spoke roughly, even to the dumb creatures, for I had a kind feeling for all. Of late (since I loved, old man), I have been cruel in my thoughts to every one. I have turned away from tenderness with bitter indifference. Listen!' she spoke in a hoarse whisper. 'I will own it. I have spoken hardly to her,' pointing towards the corpse,—'her who was ever patient, and full of love for me. She did not know,' she muttered, 'she is gone to the grave without knowing how I loved her—I had such strange, mad, stubborn pride in me.'

'Come back, mother! Come back,' said she, crying wildly to the still, solemn corpse; 'come back as a spirit or a ghost—only come back, that I may tell you how I have loved you.'

But the dead never come back.

The passionate adjuration ended in tears—the first she had shed. When they ceased, or were absorbed into long quivering sobs, David knelt down. Nest did not kneel, but bowed her head. He prayed, while his own tears fell fast. He rose up. They were both calm.

'Nest,' said he, 'your love has been the love of youth—
passionate, wild, natural to youth. Henceforward, you
must love like Christ, without thought of self, or wish for
return. You must take the sick and the weary to your
heart, and love them. That love will lift you up above the
storms of the world into God's own peace. The very
vehemence of your nature proves that you are capable of
this. I do not pity you. You do not require pity. You are
powerful enough to trample down your own sorrows
into a blessing for others; and to others you will be a
blessing. I see it before you, I see in it the answer to your
mother's prayer.'

The old man's dim eyes glittered as if they saw a vision;
the fire-light sprang up, and glinted on his long white
hair. Nest was awed as if she saw a prophet, and a
prophet he was to her.

When next David Hughes came to Pen-Morfa, he asked
about Nest Gwynn, with a hovering doubt as to the
answer. The inn-folk told him she was living still in the
cottage, which was now her own.

'But would you believe it, David,' said Mrs Thomas, 'she
has gone and taken Mary Williams to live with her? You
remember Mary Williams, I'm sure.'

No! David Hughes remembered no Mary Williams at
Pen-Morfa.

'You must have seen her, for I know you've called at John
Griffiths', where the parish boarded her?'

'You don't mean the half-witted woman—the poor crazy creature?'

'But I do!' said Mrs Thomas.

'I have seen her sure enough, but I never thought of learning her name. And Nest Gwynn has taken her to live with her.'

'Yes! I thought I should surprise you. She might have had many a decent girl for companion. My own niece, her that is an orphan, would have gone, and been thankful. Besides, Mary Williams is a regular savage at times: John Griffiths says there were days when he used to beat her till she howled again, and yet she would not do as he told her. Nay, once, he says, if he had not seen her eyes glare like a wild beast, from under the shadow of the table where she had taken shelter, and got pretty quickly out of her way, she would have flown upon him, and throttled him. He gave Nest fair warning of what she must expect, and he thinks some day she will be found murdered.'

David Hughes thought a while. 'How came Nest to take her to live with her?' asked he.

'Well! Folk say John Griffiths did not give her enough to eat. Half-wits, they tell me, take more to feed them than others, and Eleanor Gwynn had given her oat-cake, and porridge a time or two, and most likely spoken kindly to her (you know Eleanor spoke kind to all), so some months ago, when John Griffiths had been beating her, and keeping her without food to try and tame her, she

27

ran away, and came to Nest's cottage in the dead of night, all shivering and starved, for she did not know Eleanor was dead, and thought to meet with kindness from her, I've no doubt; and Nest remembered how her mother used to feed and comfort the poor idiot, and made her some gruel, and wrapped her up by the fire. And, in the morning, when John Griffiths came in search of Mary, he found her with Nest, and Mary wailed so piteously at the sight of him, that Nest went to the parish officers, and offered to take her to board with her for the same money they gave to him. John says he was right glad to be off his bargain.'

David Hughes knew there was a kind of remorse which sought relief in the performance of the most difficult and repugnant tasks. He thought he could understand how, in her bitter repentance for her conduct towards her mother, Nest had taken in the first helpless creature that came seeking shelter in her name. It was not what he would have chosen, but he knew it was God that had sent the poor wandering idiot there.

He went to see Nest the next morning. As he drew near the cottage — it was summer time, and the doors and windows were all open — he heard an angry passionate kind of sound that was scarcely human. That sound prevented his approach from being heard; and, standing at the threshold, he saw poor Mary Williams pacing backwards and forwards in some wild mood. Nest, cripple as she was, was walking with her, speaking low soothing words, till the pace was slackened, and time and breathing was given to put her arm around the crazy woman's neck, and soothe her by this tender caress into the quiet luxury of tears—tears which give the hot brain relief. Then David Hughes came in. His first words, as he took off his hat, standing on the lintel, were—'The peace of God be upon this house.' Neither he nor Nest recurred to the past, though solemn recollections filled their minds. Before he went, all three knelt and prayed; for, as Nest told him, some mysterious influence of peace came over the poor half-wit's mind, when she heard the holy words of prayer; and often when she felt a paroxysm coming on, she would kneel and repeat a homily rapidly over, as if it were a charm to scare away the Demon in possession; sometimes, indeed, the control over herself requisite for this effort was enough to dispel the fluttering burst. When David rose up to go, he drew Nest to the door.

'You are not afraid, my child?' asked he.

'No,' she replied. 'She is often very good and quiet. When she is not, I can bear it.'

'I shall see your face on earth no more,' said he. 'God bless you!' He went on his way. Not many weeks after, David Hughes was borne to his grave.

The doors of Nest's heart were opened—opened wide by the love she grew to feel for crazy Mary, so helpless, so friendless, so dependent upon her. Mary loved her back again, as a dumb animal loves its blind master. It was happiness enough to be near her. In general, she was only too glad to do what she was bidden by Nest. But there were times when Mary was overpowered by the glooms and fancies of her poor disordered brain. Fearful times! No one knew how fearful. On those days, Nest warned the little children who loved to come and play around her, that they must not visit the house. The signal was a piece of white linen hung out of a side window. On those days, the sorrowful and sick waited in vain for the sound of Nest's lame approach. But what she had to endure was only known to God, for she never complained. If she had given up the charge of Mary, or if the neighbours had risen, out of love and care for her life, to compel such a step, she knew what hard curses and blows, what starvation and misery, would await the poor creature.

She told of Mary's docility, and her affection, and her innocent, little sayings; but she never told the details of the occasional days of wild disorder, and driving insanity.

Nest grew old before her time, in consequence of her accident. She knew that she was as old at fifty as many are at seventy. She knew it partly by the vividness with which the remembrance of the days of her youth came back to her mind, while the events of yesterday were dim and forgotten. She dreamt of her girlhood and youth. In sleep, she was once more the beautiful Nest Gwynn, the admired of all beholders, the light-hearted girl, beloved by her mother. Little circumstances connected with those early days, forgotten since the very time when they occurred, came back to her mind, in her waking hours. She had a scar on the palm of her left hand, occasioned by the fall of a branch of a tree, when she was a child. It had not pained her since the first two days after the accident; but now it began to hurt her slightly; and clear in her ears was the crackling sound of the treacherous, rending wood; distinct before her rose the presence of her mother, tenderly binding up the wound. With these remembrances came a longing desire to see the beautiful, fatal well once more before her death. She had never gone so far since the day when, by her fall there, she lost love and hope, and her bright glad youth. She yearned to look upon its waters once again. This desire waxed as her life waned. She told it to poor crazy Mary.

'Mary!' said she, 'I want to go to the Rock Well. If you will help me, I can manage it. There used to be many a stone in the Dol Mawr on which I could sit and rest. We will go to-morrow morning before folks are astir.'

Mary answered briskly, 'Up, up! To the Rock Well. Mary will go. Mary will go.' All day long she kept muttering to herself, 'Mary will go.'

Nest had the happiest dream that night. Her mother stood beside her—not in the flesh, but in the bright glory of a blessed spirit. And Nest was no longer young— neither was she old—'they reckon not by days, nor years, where she was gone to dwell;' and her mother stretched out her arms to her with a calm, glad look of welcome. She awoke; the woodlark was singing in the near copse— the little birds were astir, and rustling in their leafy nests. Nest arose, and called Mary. The two set out through the quiet lane. They went along slowly and silently. With many a pause they crossed the broad Dol Mawr, and carefully descended the sloping stones, on which no trace remained of the hundreds of feet that had passed over them since Nest was last there. The clear water sparkled and quivered in the early sunlight, the shadows of the birch-leaves were stirred on the ground; the ferns—Nest could have believed that they were the very same ferns which she had seen thirty years before—hung wet and dripping where the water overflowed—a thrush chanted matins from a hollybush near—and the running stream made a low, soft, sweet accompaniment. All was the same. Nature was as fresh and young as ever. It might have been yesterday that Edward Williams had overtaken her, and told her his love—the thought of his words—his handsome looks—(he was a gray, hard-featured man by this time), and then she recalled the fatal wintry morning when joy and youth had fled; and as she remembered that faintness of pain, a new, a real faintness—no echo of the memory—came over her. She leant her back against a rock, without a moan or sigh, and died! She found immortality by the well-side, instead of her fragile, perishing youth. She was so calm and placid that Mary (who had been dipping her fingers in the well, to see the waters drop off in the gleaming sunlight), thought she was asleep, and for some time continued her amusement in silence. At last, she turned, and said,—

'Mary is tired. Mary wants to go home.' Nest did not speak, though the idiot repeated her plaintive words. She stood and looked till a strange terror came over her—a terror too mysterious to be borne.

'Mistress, wake! Mistress, wake!' she said, wildly, shaking the form.

But Nest did not awake. And the first person who came to the well that morning found crazy Mary sitting, awestruck, by the poor dead Nest. They had to get the poor creature away by force, before they could remove the body.

Mary is in Tre-Madoc workhouse. They treat her pretty kindly, and, in general, she is good and tractable. Occasionally, the old paroxysms come on; and, for a time, she is unmanageable. But some one thought of speaking to her about Nest. She stood arrested at the name; and, since then, it is astonishing to see what efforts she makes to curb her insanity; and when the dread time is past, she creeps up to the matron, and says, 'Mary has tried to be good. Will God let her go to Nest now?'

Lightning Source UK Ltd.
Milton Keynes UK
UKHW040610010320
359570UK00001B/126